Ellis Worth focused on the spill of red hair across the pillow and then broadened his attention to the rest of the writhing naked woman he'd been making love to. Her hair was a shade he'd seen on a vexing creature earlier that day. "Mary?"

Her breath caught and then her eyes widened. "You!"

Stunned, he blinked several times because he could not believe. "Mary Vine?"

"Ellis Worth," she whispered in return, covering her lips.

They stared at each other, Mary's bare chest heaving, her breasts doing lovely things underneath his clutching fingers.

HEATHER BOYD

USA TODAY BESTSELLING AUTHOR

Naughty and Nice

A Husband For Mary

DEDICATION

For Donna

"WHY CAN'T I go with you?" Mary Vine stomped her foot and instantly regretted the petulant and childish gesture she hadn't made in years. However, her brother Douglas was beyond frustrating this season. She only ever lost her sense of decorum around him.

"Because you are still a child," Douglas replied in the same condescending tone he'd adopted when he'd reached his majority last year. "The Fenwick Masquerade is no place for a properly bred young woman."

"But you go every year, and you are only a year older than me. And Worth attends, and he's younger than I am." She glanced in Mr. Ellis Worth's direction but didn't expect support from that quarter. Her brother's friend sat up suddenly, looking somewhat guilty at his inclusion in the argument. Worth was a mere week her junior and yet he could do anything he liked without his age ever being brought up in conversation.

It was not fair, and Mary hated being thwarted. She was desperately looking for a husband who would take her away from this suffocating life under her brother's stern control. The Fenwick Masquerade might be Mary's last chance to meet someone new before she was relegated to being utterly on the shelf.

Her brother sorted through the day's mail. "Worth *is* related to a duke."

Mary dismissed that argument with the wave of her hand. Worth was hardly likely to inherit that exalted position. He was very far down the line of succession and had infrequent contact with the duke. "That hardly signifies. Why can't you take me and be my chaperone for an hour?"

"We have other plans for the night."

She glanced at Ellis Worth, saw a flush of color fill his cheeks and concluded they were probably scandalous plans indeed. He squirmed under her scrutiny and looked away.

Mary was not friends with Ellis Worth. He had a terrible reputation. He was considered a rake—by Mary and many others. She tolerated him because he was unfailingly polite to her mama and had never overstepped with her. He would not help her. Only her brother could do that. She was trapped at home for yet another night unless he could be persuaded to see reason. "Please," she begged.

"Gentlemen of means do as they like, and attending Fenwick's amusements is most certainly not the place for you," Douglas remarked, smiling at an invitation in his post. "A rakish reputation only ever adds to a gentleman's esteem, but where you are concerned, attendance would make you utterly unmarriageable. Isn't that right, Worth?"

She glanced to the side again, but Worth wisely kept his mouth shut and paid strict attention to the tip of his left boot.

"Quite right," Douglas continued on, ignoring the fact he'd not been answered by his friend. "A lady should not attend such a party —or am I to believe that I have wasted considerable funds to give you this *third* season to find a spouse?"

He had her there. Mary did want, no *long,*

for a husband. She'd been searching three years, smiling at toads, suffering sweaty hands and fetid breath, inhaling the stench of too much cologne, all in the hope of finding the one man she could be herself around.

She was twenty years old and had not found the right gentleman yet. Anxiety over her spinster state had already begun to make her shrewish. Time was running out, judging by the lack of admirers adorning their drawing room today. Douglas was not keen to fund a fourth season, and she was worried. She had such high hopes the masquerade would be the answer to all her problems.

And Mary really wanted to meet a gentleman with whom she might share all sorts of adventures.

Even the wicked ones proper ladies were not supposed to think about.

Since she had not found her husband so far by being a perfect miss, she had concluded that she might have to be a little reckless to make her perfect match. What Mary wanted in a husband could not be discovered in a proper society setting. The masquerade provided ample opportunity to see a little bit of the real world, and she had so hoped Douglas would be her guide and a willing chaperone.

"Please, Douglas," she begged again. He had to help her.

"No," Douglas barked, and Mary knew better than to protest again. She turned away.

Dispirited, Mary sank down onto the chaise, ignoring her brother's conversation with Mr. Worth as they discussed the merit of attending another event that would undoubtedly exclude her too. She should have known better than to ask, but she had to try.

She was losing faith. In men, and in her own appeal. Her red hair was her most appealing feature, and her skin was flawlessly pale. She enjoyed the outdoors and exercise, but the older she got, the more times it was suggested she should not. She was afraid that her already full figure was in danger of becoming too round and unappealing. She may not have eyes to beguile an army, but she was willing to flutter her lashes a bit for the right man as long as he might make an honest woman of her in the end.

She would have to find another way to attend. She could not risk going alone. That would be madness and lead to her ruin, and yet...

The masquerade *was* tonight, on the eve of Valentine's Day, and she had everything she needed already to attend. A hooded cloak, her mother's old mask and costume, and the three gold crowns required for the entrance fee by the hosts.

Yes, she could still go even without Douglas's approval or protection, but she would have to be very brave and discreet.

"Whatever you're thinking, stop," Ellis Worth said suddenly, making her jump.

She took a deep breath, praying she'd not been talking out loud, and looked at him. He was widely considered a very handsome gentleman. Mary was not entirely immune, but she had sense enough not to fall for his charms. Ellis Worth was a heartless rogue. "What was I thinking?"

"To go without your brother's protection," he suggested in a soft voice that often caught her off guard. "I would not defy him on this."

She lifted her chin and smiled with as much frost as she could muster. "I did not ask for your opinion Mr. Worth. Should you not be with my brother rather than lingering to bother me? It is hardly proper for us to be alone together."

Mr. Worth sat forward, staring hard at Mary. "If you had been listening, you would have heard him suggest I could remain right where I am until his return at any moment. You've never complained about my company before."

True. Mary's family had never been far away when Mr. Worth came to call. He was so very wicked, but she'd always felt protected in this familiar setting. "You have never stuck your nose where it does not belong before either."

His eyes darkened. "Going to the Fenwick Masquerade won't solve your problem."

She frowned at her brother's friend. "I don't have a problem."

"The husband problem," he suggested. "Douglas believes you set your sights too high."

Douglas should have kept his opinions to himself instead of confiding in a rake like Ellis Worth. Mary straightened her spine. "No matter what my brother has suggested, my requirements for a husband are very reasonable. I am no more demanding than many young women in a similar situation."

He scowled. "You want a wealthy husband and to advance the family in society like everyone else."

Yes, wealth and good standing were important factors, but that wasn't *all* she wanted in her future. Ellis Worth would laugh if she told him she also hoped to fall in love with the man she gave her hand to. Given all she knew of a bachelor's life of excess in Town, Ellis Worth would never realize what was missing from his. She did not bother to explain. He'd hold the same opinions as her brother and dismiss her dreams of romance out of hand. She wouldn't waste her breath on so futile an explanation.

She smiled again, wishing Douglas would hurry back. "What else could be more important than making a good match?"

Worth shook his head, frowning down at his hands. "The Fenwick Masquerade offers every imaginable pleasure a body could want. Any woman there is considered equally interested in wickedness and available for the evening. You should not go. Not if you expect to make an impeccable match. The women who attend care for naught but their own pleasure. Many an innocent has been ruined by foolish dreams."

Now she really wanted to attend the Fenwick's Masquerade, but Mr. Worth did not need to know that his words of caution had fired her interest to a higher level. "I assure you, Mr. Worth, that should I require guidance, I will ask my mother and my own brother in future for their opinion and advice."

Mr. Worth pressed his lips together and then speared her with a sharp glance. "I hope you are as sensible as your words suggest."

She fanned her fingers over her chest to attempt to appear innocent. "You doubt me?"

A smile quirked his lips. "I know you."

"What does that mean?"

"You like a challenge." He glanced toward the door. "And I also know how little you think your brother cares to hear your opinion. He means well, but he's not going to suddenly see things your way. Any scandal would break your mother's heart too."

She stared at him, wondering how this man had come to know her and her family so well. To bring up her mother's heart and hopes was far too close to the truth. Mama would never find out that she went, though. "My mother wants for me what I want."

"Finding a gentleman to marry should not depend on his connections or the size of his bank account alone, as you claim. It is how he treats you that you should be more concerned about. Any man you engage in a dalliance at the masquerade could never have marriage on his mind."

Her eyes widened at the heat behind his words, and she gave up any pretense of civility between them. It was utterly reckless, but she stood and stepped closer to him. He rose to his full height, staring her down. Dear heavens, he was tall. "How dare you think you know me and what's best for me?"

"I know what it's like to be alone in the world, without family to depend on. You don't. You have everything, and you'll lose it all over a silly whim just to prove your brother a blithering idiot about a trivial ball."

Mary poked him in the chest. "Searching for a husband is not a whim, you... you... despicable rake! I never said I was going to the ball without a suitable chaperone anyway. I want to marry a man I admire. Someone I might come to love. I assure you, ladies of sense do not want a rake as a suitor. I'm not about to be tempted to throw away my life because a scoundrel smiled at me at a silly ball."

He stared at her hand on his chest until she removed it. "See that you don't."

CHAPTER TWO

DEAR GOD, Mary Vine had a temper and a sharp tongue in her head to label him a rake to his very face. He shook his head. No wonder they'd never gotten along. She would make a man miserable. The red hair on her head was a dead giveaway as to her fiery nature.

"What the devil is going on in here?" Douglas Vine demanded of them from the doorway.

Mary plastered on a false smile and then pivoted away to face her brother. "A lively debate over the foolishness of feathers as part of a man's riding costume," she told her brother in a bald-faced lie. "Worth here thinks them the height of fashion."

Ellis could care less about feathers. However, he quickly calmed himself. There was no point in stirring up trouble between the siblings. Their *discussions* could go on all day. "You misunderstood me."

"I certainly did not. I think a sensible man would never consider wearing them," she sang, her eyes just a little defiant when she glanced his way.

She flounced out of the room, and Ellis was grateful to see her go. The idea that Mary Vine wished to attend a scandalous masquerade troubled him for many reasons. First, Mary was undoubtedly an innocent young woman who hadn't a clue about the perversity of society. And second, she was clearly meant for marriage, and none of the bounders who attended Fenwick's yearly gathering were the marrying kind.

He might be the only exception.

Everything he'd said about the Fenwick Masquerade was true, and yet he still went to every ball or gathering with a glimmer of hope in his heart that somewhere in London his true love awaited him. Time was running out for him too. Mary would not find a husband at the Fenwick Masquerade, and he'd never find a wife there either. An adventurous lover perhaps but that was as far as those sorts of connections usually went.

Ellis had a problem he couldn't overcome. He wanted to marry someone who might love him for more than his link to the Duke of Levinson's seat. Until this week, the connection hadn't posed much of a hindrance to his happiness. His only source of funds was a modest inheritance that could support a small family and not much else beyond. "Are we still going to Tattersall, Mr. Vine?"

"Yes, yes," Douglas Vine agreed.

They moved to the front hall, retrieved hats and gloves, and sauntered out into the street.

After a few dozen steps, Douglas bumped his shoulder. "I apologize for my sister. She can be a silly little fool sometimes."

Douglas had no idea how bright his sister really was. Douglas Vine was one of those rare fellows who underestimated the fairer sex in general, and his sister in particular. "Don't worry about it."

"No, no. It's high time Mary learned her place and found a husband. What do you think of Woolsley?"

"A man with no sense of humor whatsoever," he said immediately. Their mutual friend bored him to tears on most days. Ellis winced. "Do we have to take him with us today?"

"I meant as a husband for Mary," Douglas suggested.

Ellis shook his head immediately. "No."

"Why not?"

Ellis laughed. "She'd walk all over him before the wedding even took place."

Douglas sighed. "I say again that you should be grateful you don't have a sister."

He would have liked a sister or a brother. He'd been alone for a long time, and he often felt lonely, even around friends. "Surely she's not so bad as all that."

Ellis may not have a family to call his own now, but he rather enjoyed spending time at the Vine household. The widowed Mrs. Vine had always been kind. He'd spent many a happy Christmas at her fireside, and looked forward to long summertime rambles in the woods in her company too.

When it came to Mary, however, he wasn't always so comfortable. She seemed to disapprove of him in general and had from the very start of their acquaintance. His reputation, and Mary's belief Ellis was a rake, meant they could never get along. They certainly could not be confidants. At least so far she seemed unimpressed by his connections. He'd never had to worry that she might see more into his visits than was there. He'd never court her. He wasn't that desperate. Mary Vine as a wife would make his life an endless nightmare, the way she carried on over every little thing.

It may not be his business, but he was still worried about their recent conversation by the time they reached Tattersalls. Mary claimed she'd not sneak away to the ball, but there was a look in her eye that hinted she was likely up to something on the sly. He'd seen that look before when her brother had adopted carrying a ridiculous walking cane to appear more worldly when he was out and about Town. Mary had not been able to hide her disapproval and had rushed outside and given it to an old gent who was hobbling past their home without the aid of one.

To this day, Vine had no idea what she'd done with the cane, and although Ellis had disapproved of her actions, he had not informed on her. She'd been young then, and impulsive in nature. However, was she impulsive enough to consider sneaking out to the ball all alone?

He sighed. Mary was not his problem. Society was. "Do you ever think you have no control over your life?"

"What are you talking about?"

"No matter what I do, people continue to make up wild stories about me. I haven't attended an entertainment this week but so far I've heard I'd seduced two innocents and a widow fresh to town without leaving my home."

"Half your luck," Vine grumbled. "There are worse things people could say about you. They could say nothing at all and barely notice you exist."

Ellis longed for that. "These rumors are getting annoying."

"You worry too much." Vine tapped his arm. "I know a dozen dull gentlemen who would kill to have your reputation with the ladies."

That reputation was getting in Ellis's way.

"What about Prescott?" Vine asked when they took seats as the first horses appeared.

Ellis liked Horace Prescott. He was a bit of a rascal with women, and even so, he was a model to Ellis's circle of friends. "He's a fine man."

"Very rich."

Money was a poor reason to marry, in his opinion. When he tried to imagine Mary happily married to Prescott, he couldn't see it. Prescott was a little too flirtatious to not be tempted by other women. Mary claimed today that she wanted to love her husband, after all. "Is he not a little old to make a match with Mary?"

"What's a few years matter if she can bring him up to scratch?"

"Twelve," he said, calculating the age gap. "He's a dozen years older than Mary. Shouldn't someone closer to her own age be a better choice?"

"Choices seem to go begging right now. Prescott will not put up with her foolishness. I think I'll invite him to dinner tomorrow night and see what happens when I leave them alone together." Vine grinned.

Ellis had been left alone, never for long, with Mary, and inevitably they only ever seemed to squabble. There must be something about his face she did not like. He changed the subject quickly. "What about that one?"

They discussed suitable mounts neither of them could afford at present before leaving after an hour in a state of ennui. The problem with horses and women was that choosing one cost a great deal of money. He wished money wasn't an issue for him, but it would define his life very soon.

"What's put you in a sour mood today?" Douglas asked suddenly as a hack neared.

Ellis waited till they were seated and underway before he shared his news. "You'll hear soon enough I suppose, but there's been a tragedy in the duke's family."

"Truly? Did one of your cousins die?"

"Both of them." That was the whole problem. His life was forever changed because two fools couldn't be bothered to learn to swim. "They drowned together because of a wager set to prove who could skull across the lake on his grace's estate. Neither one reached the shoreline to claim a victory."

Douglas Vine started to laugh. "That means you'll be a duke one day."

"Shh, keep your voice down. I'd rather no one knows for a while."

"Good God man, why? If I were next in

line to inherit a dukedom, I'd be shouting it out for all to hear."

There were many good reasons for silence. Most pressing was Ellis's desire not to feel like prey in the sights of husband-hunting women in want of a title. "It's a lot to get used to. To be honest, I'm still in shock."

"I feel for you." Douglas looked anything but concerned. The man grinned. "You'll make an excellent duke, and I'll have the pleasure of saying I knew you when you were a skinny shanked boy with no friends. Imagine the parties you can host now, eh."

He scowled at Douglas Vine, but the man only saw the benefits. Ellis's life had changed for the worse yesterday. For now, he had only a modest income, and he did not aspire to be a duke or in debt or to have a string of new friends because he was titled and wealthy. "I haven't the faintest idea how to be a duke," he confessed candidly.

"You will learn. The right sort of wife, with the right connections, will make it easier."

"Don't remind me that I must marry." Ellis slumped into his seat. "I have already endured one lecture from the duke via his solicitor. I am to wed with all possible haste and produce a dozen offspring posthaste. After me, there's no one else left to inherit, and he says I must do my duty to the family and title immediately."

Vine slapped his shoulder. "Then we'd better get you married off quick smart."

"That is not what I want."

"I'm sure every man has felt the pinch of obligation before," Douglas said, completely missing Ellis's dejection. "That does not mean your fun is over. Oh, no. Choose a wife for duty and your lovers will keep you happy elsewhere."

Douglas Vine had no idea how clueless he was. Ellis wasn't an innocent, but he certainly wasn't a rake by anyone's standards. He had encouraged the belief to avoid being teased as a young man, and the label had sadly stuck to him like glue. Even the duke had heard of it and recently lectured him on the merits of re-forming his reputation. He wasn't guilty of having done the things gossip suggested. Even with the gossip, however foolish the hope, he was still wished for a love match.

If he married for duty alone, he would never have the kind of marriage his parents had enjoyed. He remembered their happiness so well, sometimes he felt pain at their absence.

The carriage slowed. "We should celebrate your good fortune."

"My second cousins died a tragic and avoidable death," he reminded Douglas pointedly. "Celebrating it is the last thing I want to do. The eldest had a wife and three daughters. It would be an insult to them and to his memory to carry on about taking his place."

"Well, perhaps a quiet celebration is in order." Douglas pressed his hand to his heart. "I swear to be the soul of discretion. We'll gather our friends, and some lovely ladies to keep us warm, and drink until the sun rises tomorrow or the next day. What do you say?"

"I've been summoned to the duke's home tonight, unfortunately." He thought a moment. "I assumed you were attending the Fenwick Masquerade despite what you told your sister?"

Vine snorted. "I'd rather die first. There's never anyone worth having at Fenwick's."

He thought of Mary and then shoved the thought away. He'd find someone to marry who actually liked him. Him. And not the title and money coming to him eventually.

Tomorrow he'd do his duty to the family, but after he'd attended the duke's home tonight, he wanted to forget that his future was no longer his to steer. The best place to mourn the loss of his freedom was at the Fenwick annual gathering. He already had his costume, and without Douglas Vine watching, he'd be sure to have the first choice of any lady that caught his eye. "I'm sure you're right."

CHAPTER THREE

MARY WHIPPED the cloak from her shoulders and handed it off to a footman with more bravery than she'd known she possessed when she'd set out that night. Ahead of her, the world Ellis Worth had insisted she should not want to know moved and swayed with wild abandon.

But the world did not crash down on her head like he'd suggested it would.

No one pointed and stared at the virgin invading their midst. She was certainly not ruined just by being here as he'd claimed. The other guests could not know who she was anyway.

Mary was covered head to toe in her mother's old and very scandalous costume—a very long wrap bound around like a native Indian woman would wear. Her red hair was covered entirely by a dark veil of matching silk that secured across her face. To ensure her identity remained a secret, she'd carefully dabbed her pale brows with dark kohl to hide the shade. She was utterly unrecognizable, even to herself almost.

She was drawn into the nearest crowded room, fascinated by a side of life her family had shielded her from to the best of their ability. But she had known such revels existed. They were whispered of, overheard. Douglas and Ellis Worth were frequent participants.

There was an abundance of merriment, dancing, and loud laughter around her almost immediately. Farther in, she caught sight of a man nibbling at a woman's throat, and she stopped, appalled that the lady allowed it and made no move to stop him doing it.

Surely she wasn't the only one to think it scandalous.

Mary glanced around, but no one paid any attention. It was as if such behavior was allowed, overlooked by everyone around the couple.

Embarrassed and uncomfortable, she

averted her eyes and went in search of other less salacious sights.

What she found in the next room was the most beautiful man in existence.

She'd danced with her share of lesser creatures, but this scantily clad fellow took her breath away. She moved for a closer look at his scandalous garb.

He was tall, his dark hair peeking out from beneath a golden masked helmet at the nape, but what he wore below his jaw made her mouth suddenly so very moist. She swallowed and drew closer, unable to stop herself from staring.

He wore leather sandals on his otherwise bare feet with ties crisscrossed up his muscular calves. Around his hips he wore a short scrap of white linen that left little to the imagination, trimmed with gold braid and so thin, Mary could almost make out the top of his thighs. A heavier pleated sash, similar to Scottish garb of old but white, draped over one perfectly bronzed shoulder. The garment, if it could be called that, flowed loosely around his broad chest, leaving very little of his torso hidden from view or to her imagination. After studying him a few moments, a great many questions had been answered concerning what men looked like beneath their very proper dress.

"He may as well be naked," she whispered to herself, then slapped her hand over her mouth. Not that anyone can hear her whisper over the din.

If he had been naked, then the last of her questions about the male of the species might be answered in one evening.

The man toyed with a gilt-handled sword idly, swinging the blade as if the silvered edge was utterly harmless as he watched the crowd around him with restless interest. He seemed to be alone. Perhaps the weapon was harmless, but undoubtedly so handsome a man could not be.

The muscles of his back and strong arms flexed as he shifted position, revealing a lean, muscular frame that made her pulse race. Mary licked her lips, astounded by her reaction to him. She was becoming quite warm and restless too as she looked upon his spectacular form with no idea what to do about it.

Oh, how she wished they could be introduced. Mary was alone, and so was he. However, a masked ball was a place of anonymity so the pleasure of his name would have to wait. She would have to stir her courage to have the pleasure of his company, even if the idea of it turned her stomach into very tight knots.

When he turned, their eyes met, and she couldn't look away for a full minute. She did glance away eventually, blushing furiously under her veil. What was she doing? She'd never been so captivated before by a man, let alone a stranger in a crowded room. She had come tonight to broaden her knowledge of the real world. Gawking at a beautiful man, no matter how fascinating, wasn't all she was here to do.

She was looking for a man who might marry her too.

She took a step but a scantily clad male chest materialized before her, halting her progress. Since she'd just studied that chest from afar, she found proximity to the curves and bulges of muscle all the more disconcerting up close.

His deep, masculine voice caught her by surprise too. "Devi?"

She glanced up, into the bright eyes of the stranger sparklingly with barely concealed mirth. The man thought she was a *goddess.* Who was she to deny him the delusion? Yet she felt an instant connection and smiled at him. "Centurion?"

"At your service." He bowed elegantly, deeply, and she was smitten anew by the way he moved. "Are you lost, Devi?"

"How could I be lost with such a warrior before me," she replied in a huskier tone than she usually spoke in, blushing furiously at her deception. Mary shouldn't have responded to him like this, but since her argument with Ellis Worth, Mary was feeling rather bold. She fluttered her lashes a little.

He extended his hand, and Mary placed hers upon his broad and bare palm. Awareness of him rushed over her senses. Her breasts grew heavy under his warm stare. She lifted her chin, leaning toward him. "A pleasure to make your acquaintance."

"It could be." He dipped toward her, his grin widening. "I humbly offer my escort, for a dance or to any quarter of the known world that provides amusement, if that is your desire."

Her desires would get her into trouble.

Suddenly, Mary did not care. "Lead the way, Centurion."

He squeezed her hand, and it felt right to let him escort her around the unfamiliar home and entertain her with his charming wit and generous laughter for the next hour. There was something about him, some swift and unknown symmetry that had brought him to her notice and kept him at her side. Who was she to deny fate?

He passed her champagne when a footman carried a tray past and smiled down at her as she sipped the strange liquid. A warm glow filled her with longing to know him, every time he smiled, her resolve to be careful diminished a little more. Where had this man been all her life? She had to find out who he was. "Do you know our hosts well?"

"I know them as well as anyone who made it past the butler."

Drat! That meant he could be someone important or a nobody with funds to spare. Their hosts did not discriminate against rank or reputation. Money and connections were all very well but never made up for the lack of character.

"How well do you know them?" he asked suddenly.

"Oh, not at all." Mary turned her face away, hiding a blush. She had to be careful to find out who he was before she risked her own identity being revealed. "They are very brave to open their home to so many strangers. Do the Fenwick's not fear being robbed?"

"Everything of value is locked away." He nodded to a group nearby. "They hire additional servants, men and women costumed to blend in, to ensure the peace and order are maintained."

A couple, perched precariously on a chair, toppled off nearby and onto the floor, laughing but not halting their amorous pursuits. "They're not doing a very good job of it," she suggested dryly to her escort.

The pair wrestled around, sucking at each other's lips with utter abandon while everyone looked on.

The centurion laughed and leaned close again. "The trick there would have been to find a sturdier chair, or perhaps make use of a bedchamber upstairs."

"Surely our hosts would not permit that," she said, unable to hide her surprise.

"Anything is possible on a night like this." He winked. "A goddess may have anything she desires. She need only offer the right encouragement to be worshiped."

Mary blushed hotly beneath her veil as a waltz was struck up by the orchestra playing somewhere above their heads on the balcony. She'd been secretly taught the steps by her dance instructor, but rarely danced it due to its scandalous reputation and Douglas's disapproval. She would like to dance tonight, and her brother was not here to see her do it.

She'd like to dance all night with her handsome centurion, if such a feat could be managed. At two dances, it would be assumed she and her centurion had an understanding if they were in any other place of entertainment. For the first time in her life, she wanted to flout the rules and live very dangerously indeed.

She leaned close to her companion. "Dance with me."

His lips curved up into a delighted smile. "I was just about to ask, but I'll dance with you all night if you would allow me the pleasure."

"I think I will." She curled her arm

through his and smiled. Yes, she would be very reckless indeed and enjoy her handsome companion. "Lead the way, sir."

The centurion was an excellent dancer. Every brush of their hands, smile exchanged made her heart ache to be closer to him. Mary could not stop caressing the bulge of his shoulder muscle whenever the chance came, and he allowed it, encouraged her touch even with his frequent smiles. His body was so distracting that blushing had almost become second nature.

They danced four dances together, something that would be terribly improper anywhere else, and at the end of the fourth set he led her toward the refreshment table and handed her another glass of champagne to cool her down.

She was not just hot from the dancing. All her senses seemed heightened in his company. "Lovely," she whispered.

"Yes, you are." He eased her away from the refreshment table, his hand warm on her back and sending tingles all over her body. "It has been a memorable evening."

"Indeed." Mary peeked at him. He was so perfect for her in every way that mattered that she was afraid for a moment that he might not feel the same. What would happen if he was merely toying with her affections? How would she even know? "I don't want tonight to end yet," she murmured.

"Neither do I." His arm firmed around her back, pulling her close against his warm chest. "Stay with me," he whispered.

Mary blushed and leaned into him while she caught her breath. Her pulse raced at his proximity yet she had no desire to distance herself from him as a proper lady should. She hadn't found a husband in three seasons, her fourth might never happen, but she was utterly enthralled by this stranger. Aroused by his smiles, and by his touch. She hadn't the faintest idea who he might be and it didn't seem important. Tonight was her only chance to experience passion and she would take a chance on him. "Can I?"

"Yes, Devi," he said then leaned closer, allowing her to touch his face. "I want you more than anything in the world."

Mary glanced around at the other guests. She wished they were alone so she could have this one night of uninterrupted bliss with him without witnesses. "Where can we go?"

His lips caressed her ear. "I am sure we could find a private chamber upstairs if you'd care to explore the rest of the house together."

A bedchamber seemed a very good idea if she was going to be truly wicked. She felt a little too exposed here. She curled her arm about his, breathless with anticipation, and held onto him tightly. "I'd like to be alone with you."

They burst into an unoccupied room with a groan half an hour later, finally having made an escape from the crowds below and avoided the other lovers making use of dark corner of house. What she had seen already had given her imagination a great many ideas of how to pass the rest of her evening. Her heart had been well and truly lost to the centurion.

Tearing at their clothes in their eagerness to touch each other, now they could not be seen by others, disapproving or applauding, they slammed the door shut, leaving them in near darkness.

A quick glance revealed they'd stumbled into a bedchamber. Mary backed toward the bed, legs a little weak, beckoning her handsome centurion to follow with her fingers. His grin grew as he dropped his costume from his broad shoulders right at the door.

Mary did not bother to hide her sigh of appreciation. Her centurion was indeed handsome and well formed from head to toe. She admired his body, allowing her eyes to rest on his manhood as it thickened and rose. She blinked at his increasing proportions and then licked her lips, discovering now the last piece of her questions had been answered. This is what made men and women different. This was how men and women made children. That was how they came together in bed. "Oh my!"

"Do I please you, Devi?"

"Yes," she said breathlessly. She slipped her gown off one shoulder as her breasts grew heavy yet again. Her nipples had become so sensitive they tingled. She had a feeling this man would know how to fix that.

The centurion caught the end of her garment and Mary gracefully unwound the abnormally long length from her body by turning slowly around until she was naked. Her costume left no room for chemise or stays, so she stood nervously until her centurion's grin grew wide. "Exactly my thought about you. Your skin, your body, is beyond compare." He cupped her jaw, and his fingers found the fastening of her veil. "I would grant your heart's desire in an instant should you confess it is me."

His words made her brave, to ask for what they'd been rushing toward since she'd met him. "Make love to me."

"Gladly, Devi." His fingers teased softly around her neck as he brought his lips close to hers. She shivered, but not from the cold when he whispered, "My love. Forever."

He crushed her mouth under his, teasing his tongue into her mouth with delicate and deliberate sweeps, the like of which she'd never expected but instinctively craved more of. Desire awakened her yearning as he caressed her bare skin, skimming so gently down her back that she never wanted him to stop touching her. She backed toward the bed, drawing her masked lover with her.

When the bed touched the back of her thighs, he lifted her up and sat her upon the coverlet to remove her slippers. "You won't be needing these for a while."

He kissed her toes, toyed with the bells fastened to her ankles, then struggled out of his own laced sandals before following her onto the bed.

He rested his body over hers without crushing her, but there was no escape from the fact she was in bed with a man she did not know but wanted with all her heart and soul. She was spellbound by his warmth and the tantalizing brush of his skin and erection against her body.

She wrapped her arms around his neck and pulled him down for a deep kiss. She couldn't contemplate stopping. Not when she felt like this. He was everything she wanted and more. Tonight she would experience passion and hope it would be enough.

He fondled her breasts, and she pushed up her chest into the erotic sensation. He had lovely large hands and seemed to like her body as much as she liked his. His mouth settled over one peak, and he sucked and kissed them, groaning a little. "Perfect."

"Yes," she held him close. "Perfect."

"There's plenty of time for everything, but..." he whispered as he took her hand and pressed it against his arousal.

Mary sighed. Last question answered. She felt him, explored him and knew she would like being this man's wife very much if his intentions were honorable.

Mary's hair covering caught beneath her and she tugged off the hair piece at precisely the same moment as he removed his helmet.

ELLIS WORTH FOCUSED on the spill of red hair across the pillow and then broadened his attention to the rest of the writhing naked woman he'd been making love to. Her hair was a shade he'd seen on a vexing creature earlier that day. "Mary?"

Her breath caught and then her eyes widened. "You!"

Stunned, he blinked several times because he could not believe. "Mary Vine?"

"Ellis Worth," she whispered in return, covering her lips.

They stared at each other, Mary's bare chest heaving, her breasts doing lovely things underneath his clutching fingers. Her hips jerked hard against his and all of a sudden her sex cradled the tip of his erection.

Time slowed, but his ardor cooled a little more with each tortured breath he took.

He'd been about to...

They'd been about to...

He was right there, ready to plunge into bliss, to claim his own goddess. His own sweet love forevermore, never knowing he was kissing his best friend's little sister.

Mary scrambled back at the same moment he made the same decision to retreat. "How could you?" Mary exclaimed, tugging at the coverlet beneath them in a bid to cover her beautiful, lush body.

He gaped, but didn't move to aid her. "How could I what? How could *you*? I certainly did not imagine the wild and wanton woman who dragged me up here could be my best friend's sister. What kind of game are you playing to torment me so?"

"My game? I think not." Still trapped by his proximity, Mary stretched for the pieces of her costume, which were strewn about the bed they'd just (almost) made love on. She held the fine cloth over her breasts tightly, an action that revealed their loveliness as she pushed them up higher. His breath caught but he fought his desire. "You knew it was me.

You knew I would attend. How cruel of you to trick me."

"Trick you? I believed you would keep your word and stay at home." He sat back on his heels in consternation. Ruining Mary had not been his plan, but then again, he'd barely enjoyed a rational thought from the moment their eyes had met in the ballroom downstairs. He'd felt an instant connection to her and un-deniable attraction. She'd *flirted* with him. *Mary* had pursued him! "You knew I was in-vited tonight and I think you must have known it was me all along and this is your re-venge. I'm not that different in the dark."

One delicately arched dark eyebrow rose high. "You were pleasant to me. You encour-aged me to like you."

He spluttered out a curse that would likely burn her ears, but under the circum-stances, he could not summon up the least bit of guilt over it. He felt utterly betrayed and exposed. He glanced around, fearing he was about to be set up to compromise Mary and be forced to marry her. He would one day be wealthy and titled. However, he couldn't marry Mary. Not when she disliked him so much. "Please remember it was not me who kissed first. You, Mary Vine, all but threw yourself at me tonight."

"And you accepted without even knowing my name," she whispered with a horrified glance at his bare body. "You *are* the rake everyone claims you to be, after all."

He crawled forward, furious, and hovered over her, determined there should be no mis-understandings between them now. "You put your lips to mine first and all but dragged me off a dance floor and up to this room so we could make love. I'm only guilty of being a willing participant in your debauchery, swept away by your passion, and nothing more de-vious than that. I never planned this. I would not do such a low deed. You are my best friend's sister. I never once dreamed your kisses would taste so sweet and that I would be smitten. I never imagined I could desire...*you*."

"Smitten?" She blinked, and did not deny her culpability in the matter. But she did push him back, her tiny hands torture on his over-sensitive skin. "I would not have kissed you if I'd known who you really were," she confessed. "I don't trust you, and I'd hardly want a man that behaved as you do."

Despite the insult leveled against him, he breathed a little easier, feeling almost certain he wasn't about to fall victim to a parson's trap.

"I'm sure I would not have kissed you either. What was it you said to me, half a day ago it must have been? Let me see. *Ladies of sense do not want a rake as a suitor*," he bit out, quoting her slight of earlier that day back at her. "How dare you label me a rake and then seduce me yourself! Douglas told you about me. You speak so proudly of your own propriety but act just like everyone else."

"Of course he told me all about you. You're a rake, and I wasn't going to fall into your arms for no good reason."

He laughed at his own naivety. "You most definitely flirted with me. I should have suspected even you'd be willing to get into my trousers now."

Her lips pursed in an expression he knew well. She was winding up for a good argument. "I most certainly did not," she said insisted. "You were not wearing trousers *in the first place!*"

He drew back, surprised by the humor of her words, but still bitterly disappointed. How sad that they could get along well but only when they didn't recognize each other. Mary would never think kindly of him after this debacle. He should hardly expect her understanding for going along with a seduction with a woman he'd never bothered to learn the real name of.

However, it might be a near miss for her virtue, but thankfully no real damage was done to her innocence. Mary would quickly forget his hands peeling her out of her clothes in a day or two, or how he'd caressed her fair, delicate skin tenderly, skimming heaven in preparation for an explosive passion of the like he'd never once imagined existed.

Ellis, however, would have trouble purging from his mind how heatedly they'd come together with so little provocation. He'd thought he'd met his goddess tonight and had eyes for no one else since. They'd gotten quite carried away with their flirtation without a clue as to their real identities. He hadn't recognized her voice over the noise of the crowd. But he'd seen her instant lust and willingness while they'd danced, and responded to her honestly with his own.

He regarded her warily, confused by her as feelings of protectiveness rose up even now. She should not be here. Outside were any number of rascals who would not have stopped short of satisfying themselves with her. She was lucky she'd picked him out of the crowd to seduce. At least he had honor enough to do the right thing and stop, now that their disguises were off. "You must go home."

Still clutching the costume to her breasts, she fumbled with the ends, flashing him a glimpse of her nipple, the curve of her waist. She stared at herself and then hugged the garment tightly to her chest. "I can't."

"For God's sake, Mary, do you want to be found like this? You can't possibly remain without a chaperone."

She dropped her chin. "I know that too."

She buried her face in her hands and sobbed quite pitifully.

Ellis ground his teeth and cautiously approached. He hated it when women resorted to tears to make a man feel bad about a situation. He never knew what to do, and he wasn't the only one to blame, or be upset about it. Mary had been so very intent on having him that it never crossed his mind to refuse her advances or question her real identity first.

She cried softly, bitterly, and he sank down beside her on the edge of the bed. Guilt was the harshest master for a gentleman of honor, and he set one hand on her knee to gain her attention. "I'm sorry that you ended up like this with me."

She smacked his hand away. "I'm not crying over you, you horrible man. I cannot dress in this contraption without help. As soon as I call for a maid, everyone will know how stupid I was tonight. I will be found out no matter what I do next."

He pursed his lips and then nodded when the only logical solution that would prevent scandal came to him. "Since I got you out of the costume, perhaps you'd permit me to re-dress you."

She scowled at him, her tears instantly replaced by irritation. They stared at each other, and heat burned between them. But not just anger. Beneath it all, lust remained. He felt it as surely as if they were touching. And he wasn't the only one suffering the malady of disappointment either. Mary licked her lips, her attention sweeping across his chest too. He ached to lean forward to claim her lips again. They parted, and Mary's languid gaze drew him in. Ellis was almost upon her, almost kissing her, when her tiny hand slapped over his heart. "Don't you dare kiss me, Ellis Worth!"

"You didn't mind earlier," he pointed out but drew back as asked. "You shouldn't look at me like you want to eat me if you don't expect me to think about doing the same to you."

She turned her face away and closed her eyes. "Scoundrel."

"Guilty earlier tonight. Now, I will behave because you want me to. Let me help us both escape this mistake with as much dignity as possible. I promise I will resist your come-hither looks in future and keep my unreasonable desire for you under control, since you dislike me so very much."

He tugged the garment from her soft hands, ignoring her frowning face, and shook it out briskly. It was badly wrinkled but whole. In his haste to reach the bed, he was glad to see he'd not utterly destroyed her costume.

He did have a good recollection of its twists and turns from undressing her, which of course made him recall what he'd found beneath. Mary Vine was such a contradiction he couldn't yet reconcile the two sides of her. One moment more passionate than he deserved, the next cutting and hostile. He much preferred the former attributes. She fair took his breath away with her passions. He'd love to kiss her again one day, press his mouth to her crisp red curls between her legs and make her scream out in pleasure.

His breath caught, his pulse hammered through his veins, and desire affected his manhood yet again. Kissing Mary had been intoxicating. Touching her, bliss. He swallowed hard, wishing tonight could have ended in an entirely different manner and turned away. They'd been so close. He'd even briefly believed he'd found his true love at last. "In case I never get the opportunity to speak frankly again, you are a breathtaking and passionate woman. You will make some gentleman a very lucky bastard when you marry him."

There was silence behind him a long moment. "Thank you, I think."

Ellis ran his hands through his hair,

cursing his poor luck and expecting more to come. He'd have to escort Mary home to ensure she was protected from further unwanted advances. He could not in good conscience allow her to travel London's streets alone. But what would happen if her family discovered them together at his hour?

Douglas would demand a marriage. He'd be pleased that Mary would become a duchess one day. Mary might hate him for taking away her chance of happiness, but Ellis would offer her his name. It was the least he could do under the circumstances. Ellis was too much of a gentleman to abandon her to face scandal alone. If there were no other way to salvage her reputation, he would do the honorable thing and marry her immediately, even if it meant he'd be miserable right alongside her too for the rest of their lives.

He turned, offered a wry smile, hoping there was a way to salvage the situation and not end up the bitterest of almost bedfellows. She might not like him right now, but he'd always thought her clever and very much a lady worthy of respect for all her impulsive ways.

He waited patiently for her to stand. However, Mary Vine remained wrapped up in the coverlet, regarding him with her head tipped slightly to the side and her lips parted. She appeared dazed again.

"You'll have to come out of there for me to be of any help," he reminded her.

She remained still. Staring at Ellis, so he returned her scrutiny, admiring how lovely she looked in a passion-tossed bed, red hair wild across her pale shoulders. She would be utterly naked when she came out of there, and he suddenly covered his groin with his hands as his cock pulsed with arousal.

He was naked now and on display...with a rampant erection bobbing between them, reminding her of what they'd been about to do together.

His cock thickened further, despite any attempt to explain to it that the woman, a virgin with her eyes wide open now, did not want anything to do with him unless it was to further her ambition to marry well.

He turned away, grabbed his Roman costume, and tossed one scrap of fabric around his hips. There hadn't been much to his costume. Sadly, evidence of his arousal remained, jutting out beneath the flimsy garb.

"My apologies," he muttered, realizing

that his nakedness might have stunned her into immobility. Tonight was probably the first time she'd ever seen a man without clothes, let alone an aroused one. When they'd walked the ballroom below, she has been so fascinated by the hair on his arms that she'd actually stroked him. Her touch had been heavenly. Given the way she continued to stare now, her fascination with the male form had not ended with the revelation of his identity.

But whether it was to his benefit or detriment, he couldn't say.

Once he was more or less properly attired, Mary stretched one slender leg from beneath the comforter and stood. The coverlet fell away slowly, revealing her breasts, generous hips, and the bright patch of curls hiding her sex. Gods, he'd nestled the head of his cock right there before sanity had returned.

He swallowed hard, shoving away his remaining lust, as she bravely stepped toward him without a stitch of cloth hiding her charms, her arms rising to aid in her dressing, causing her breasts and bells to jiggle. *Hell.* She was more beautiful, more of a temptation than she could possibly know. His hands shook as he began to wind the fabric from her left hip and around and around. Her nipples had hardened by the time he looped the fabric up and over her shoulder. He could see them jutting out at him as they had before they'd come upstairs.

Ellis still wanted to make love to Mary Vine.

Surely the pleasure of kissing her sense-less again could be worth the risk of an un-happy match. Mary had seemed to like him very much before, but he'd not imagined their attraction tonight. It might seem implausible that Mary had wanted to do wicked things *with* him, and their bodies clearly had their own agendas still.

He finished dressing Mary, frowning as his thoughts veered from flight from the situa-tion or fight for a second chance to win her over. When they were decent, he led her through the throbbing mass of debauchery in the halls and ballrooms, doing his best to shield her from the worst of the sin on display, and returned her home without another word about what they'd almost done together.

However, he could not stop thinking of how much he'd enjoyed their reckless evening, and whether or not she would escape the scandal they'd made together. As they parted ways in her garden, he had a sudden selfish wish that she'd be caught, and that she would send for him to make things right.

CHAPTER FIVE

DAYBREAK ONLY WORSENED Mary's impending sense of doom. She'd kissed Ellis Worth. Kissed him, touched him, pressed her bare body to his and proved herself a woman of low and utterly alarming morals. Ellis had pretty much dubbed her the female equivalent of a rake, and he might be right. That he'd not finished the job of ensuring her ruin was gratifying and yet unsettling.

She punched her pillow. For a rake, Ellis was not living up to his reputation for seduction.

Oh, his kisses had been very fine.

More than fine.

Mary pressed her pillow to her face and growled her frustration into the feathers.

He was exceptionally good at kissing, and other things. Things he'd not wanted to continue once he'd discovered her real identity. It was so very lowering to be cast aside so swiftly because of who she was and not because of how she felt in his arms.

She flipped over to her back but turned her head toward the window to watch the bright day begin. Ellis was Douglas's best friend. They saw each other practically every day. Ellis would come to call on Douglas, not her, and she'd be forced to watch him from afar, knowing what lay beneath his clothes and that she'd fooled herself into thinking him the love of her life for a very brief time last night.

What sane woman could love a rake?

Her breath caught. *Mary* might have if given a chance.

It might amuse others to imagine bringing such a man to his knees and hearing a sweet proposal tumble from his lips, but Ellis Worth was the last person to ever consider falling in love. Certainly not with her, and never now that he'd seen her true colors.

Last night had been all her fault.

She had tried to seduce him, she'd led him

on, absolutely kissed him first. She could not deny his accusations because they cut so very close to the bone. Everything he'd claimed about her behavior was utterly true. For a supposedly virtuous woman, she was decidedly *not* when faced with the temptation of his powerful and naked body.

He was beautiful. Arousing. Desirable.

Oh, she was utterly ruined now. Mary pulled her pillow over her head as her face burned with the heat of a blush, remembering how he'd made her *feel* him with her hand. She would not be able to look at him now without remembering how much she had wanted to experience his love and desire. It had almost hurt to draw back from the brink.

Tap, tap, tap.

Mary sprung up at the knocks on her door, brushing her hair from her face and then clutching her pillow for scant reassurance. "I'm awake."

Her mother hurried in, wearing her nightgown and lacy cap still perched on her head. "Oh good. You must get up. There is a caller."

"Who?"

"Mr. Worth has come."

"Worth always comes on Tuesdays," she

said in what she hoped was a disinterested tone, although a dull roar had filled her ears at the mention of his name. Fear and excitement affected her. Usually, she felt resignation whenever he came to call.

One night, and so much had changed between them.

"He's much too early." Mama hurried to Mary's wardrobe and selected a modest lemon gown. "Tolling warned that Mr. Worth appeared quite formal. He did not smile even once, and that is so unlike him. Douglas appears out, too, though your brother never mentioned an early appointment to anyone. It is rude since he must have known Worth would call as he always does on Tuesdays. You must go down in his place. I beg of you to entertain Mr. Worth before he takes himself off in a dreadful huff."

Mary slipped from the bed, heart pounding in dread. Had he come to reveal her wickedness and disobedience to her family? She had to prevent that by any means. She'd be sent to live with her grandmamma in disgrace for what she'd done last night if he had. If that happened, she'd never marry, she'd never be kissed so fiercely and be made weak by Ellis's expert passions yet again.

She blinked to clear that wicked remembrance from her mind. She should not wish for another interlude like last night. But oh how his strong hands had grasped her desperately before their identities had changed everything. He'd made her feel utterly desirable. And yet...

Mary shook her head. Ellis was not here for her, nor would he ever attempt to kiss her. She should not allow the rake any further liberties, even if she wanted them. He was merely here to see Douglass, as he always did on Tuesday mornings, and she would endure this visit the way she had borne all the others.

"I will see him," she promised. "And explain."

She hurried through her toilette, choosing a prettier gown than her mother had laid out, and rushed downstairs, her nerves jumping chaotically. What would he say to her? How should she greet him? Like sworn enemies, though perhaps a little less hostility would be a good start if she wanted to ensure he said nothing about last night.

Mary swept into the drawing room and stopped short when she saw him.

Ellis Worth took her breath away.

Too elegantly dressed to be meeting Douglass for a trip to Tattersall's, too handsome for words indeed. It took her a full minute to get over the shock of seeing him dressed because she remembered so much of last night, when he was anything but proper to look at. The heat of his skin, the heaviness of his body pressing hers into the mattress, the skill of his lips and hands as they moved over her own.

She belatedly remembered her manners and fumbled a poor curtsy, blushing furiously under his scrutiny. "Sir?"

His eyes glowed with something warm and wicked stirring in their depths when she met his gaze. "Miss Vine, good morning."

Mary rushed across the room and, in her haste, stumbled into a chair instead of settling elegantly. She straightened herself out in a wink and offered Ellis Worth a tentative smile that she hoped did not reveal how truly nervous she was to see him. "I'm afraid you've caught the family unprepared this morning. Douglas has already gone out."

"Or hasn't returned yet," he murmured

under his breath. "Mornings are not his favorite time of day."

She frowned at Ellis. "And knowing this, you came so early?"

"What can I say, I like to live dangerously."

He smiled, and her lips twitched similarly in a response she could barely control. Last night, before she had known she was conversing with Ellis, she had enjoyed his whispered confidences and flirtatious remarks. He'd made her laugh so often that her cheeks had ached. Too bad that could not continue. A rake did not suddenly become safe or respectable. "So you do."

Despite her anxiety in his presence, he made himself comfortable, crossing one leg over the other as if he planned to stay awhile. Mary dragged her attention back to his face. "I trust you are in good spirits."

He tilted his head to the side and his gaze dropped down to her feet and rose slowly. "The Fenwick Masquerade was quite..."

"Amusing?" she suggested, fearing his description.

"Stimulating would be a better description," he murmured with a quirk of his lips. "I had no idea an hour or two could change my opinion so profoundly."

She stared at his lip when he took one between his teeth. Mary cleared her throat as her body reacted to him with so little provocation. "You did say it was a scandalous gathering. I imagine a rake would be used to that sort of thing by now."

"There are some things a man is never prepared for." He wrinkled his nose. "Let me ask you something. Are you aware that your brother was once chased out of his lover's bed three times in one week because the husband kept coming home unexpectedly early?"

She frowned. "My brother? I thought that was *you* running away."

"That's what I feared you'd say." He shook his head, his face becoming serious. "It hit me like a blow to the head last night that someone must have been telling you tall tales about my life. For your information, I've had exactly three brief affairs. Despite the rumors, none of the ladies had living husbands at the time."

She closed her eyes, unhappy to hear about the other women he'd successfully bedded. What he did in his private life mattered nothing to her, except that what he claimed did not match his rakish reputation. She would not be so easily fooled by some sweet words today. She knew all about his amorous exploits from gossip. She opened her eyes. "I supposed you did not swim naked in the Serpentine last year either?"

"Ah, so you heard about that too, did you?" He laughed. "Barefooted to my knees, and it was bloody cold I will tell you. Your brother dropped something, and I was a good friend and went in to fetch it."

"You disparage my brother?" She licked her lips. They should not be speaking of these things, but it bothered her that he would lie even now. "It was said your married lover dared you to prove your devotion by swimming across."

"Such foolishness. No wonder you think as ill of me as the duke does. You've both been grossly misinformed." He snorted. He sat forward suddenly, arms resting on his thighs as he stared into her eyes. "Ask me anything, and I promise to tell you the truth."

"What you do is none of my concern."

"Oh, but it is. Your good opinion matters more than anything else now. I have struggled to understand why you do not like me, and I can see gossip has colored your understanding of my character."

Mary frowned. "I know what everyone knows."

"Not quite. You have always thought ill of me, even though I did nothing untoward. I fear you've been privy to malicious rumors of my so-called indiscretions. Who has filled your ears with these lies? Tell me? A friend obviously, since you do not question their intelligence."

Mary shook her head. "I warn my friends away from you. They'd never want to marry a rake, no matter what they say to the contrary."

He brushed aside her confession of tattling on him to her friends with the wave of his hand. "So, not a friend, but someone close to you, perhaps even closer than friendship? Family?"

Mary swallowed, suddenly made nervous by the direction of his questions. They were a little too close to the truth for comfort.

His jaw clenched suddenly, and he turned his face away for a long moment. Mary detected a soft curse slip from his lips that made her blush. He rubbed his hand over his mouth and turned back to her, eyes dull. Bleak. She was more than a little taken aback by his swift change of expression. It seemed all the joy she'd seen dancing in their depths last night had been wiped from his features. "Ellis, what is it?"

"It is as I suspected, but I still do not understand why he lied to you about me." He stretched one hand toward her then jerked it back as if he'd not meant to reach for her. "I promise you, I am not the rake you have been led to believe. I'll prove it to you now."

"How?"

He stood, strolled quietly toward the open door, and peered out into the hall. He pushed the door closed a little more then returned to his spot. "I came to see how you fared after our adventure, and to discover if I had imagined last night. I am relieved beyond words that nothing has changed," he whispered so low she almost couldn't hear him.

He sat forward on his chair, so close to the edge that he was almost falling out of it as he continued in a softer tone, "If I were a rake, I wouldn't have come. I wouldn't have lost an entire night of sleep worrying about how you might feel this morning. If I were the cold-hearted scoundrel, I would have moved on to my next conquest, the next woman, and been done with you. But I cannot do that. Not after last night. I feel responsible. That is why I'm here so early, too early to see Douglas. I couldn't stay away. I have to know that you do not hate me. I could not bear it if you thought me a villain. I came for you, Mary."

Mary gasped, utterly surprised by Ellis's impassioned declaration. He was sincerely worried. She could see it in his eyes. Hear it in his tone. He honestly cared about her, and the possibility of her ruin was not what he hoped for. How very unlike the rake she'd expected to be faced with today.

Mary glanced toward the door quickly, profoundly affected by his words. She would set his mind to rest that no harm had come following her adventure last night, but she also desperately hoped her mother would stay away a little bit longer. "Mama sleeps very soundly," she whispered. "I had no explanations to make about last night. Douglas, well, as I said, he stayed out. I don't hate you, but I was shocked to discover it was you I'd kissed, and more so by my own forward behavior. I don't know what come over me."

"I *do* understand, though I prefer that you never apologize for what happened between us. Nothing you did with me was wrong as far as I'm concerned. Those unguarded hours with you is an interlude I will always treasure no matter what happens in my life." He drew in a deep breath. "I will not make excuses for my behavior afterward. I knew immediately what was the right thing to do, and I let our history still my tongue."

She frowned. Ellis had been understandably angry at first, but she'd thought him very kind to help her make her escape. He had no reason to aid her. "I was equally to blame. I..."

"Do let me continue." Ellis slid to his knees on the rug before Mary and smiled up at her. He took her hand gently in his and stroked his thumb across the back of her glove in a soft caress.

She was swept back to the evening before, attracted to him, aroused by his touch and his intensity. Something she'd never experienced with him in any other setting. Sparks of lust traveled up her arm and coiled around her body until she almost couldn't breathe. "Please do," she whispered in a horrifyingly husky tone.

"This may be too soon, and you may need time to consider my request, but Mary Vine, would you do me the honor of accepting my hand in marriage?" Ellis asked before leaning forward to brush his lips across hers.

____

CHAPTER SIX

MARY KISSED HIM BACK. She couldn't help it. Mary couldn't stop herself stealing one more improper moment with the handsome, irresistible Ellis Worth. She touched his face, eager to never halt the madness consuming her soul. She'd gone to the masquerade hoping for adventure, and here it was, right where she'd never dreamed of finding it.

"Devi," he whispered against her lips, skimming his hand up her side to touch her head.

She drew back to stare at him. To see the expression in his eyes that had sent her pulse flying last night. They were so close, nothing else seemed more important than him. She had so much to tell him, to explain...

Heavy footsteps pounded down the stairs, breaking her daze.

Ellis flew back into his seat with a softly uttered curse. Mary faced the door, a blush warming her cheeks at nearly being caught kissing a man she'd known and dismissed for years. She had no words to describe the state of her heart. She did not know whether to accept or decline Ellis Worth's most flattering offer of matrimony.

She needed time to think.

Marriage had not been expected when she'd woken that morning.

She'd never imaged Ellis would ask for her hand, or ask in such an un-rake like way. He had looked almost happy to make the offer.

Her brother burst into the room a moment later. Douglas glanced between them. "Don't say you're still arguing over wretched feathers?"

"No more disagreements here. I revised my opinion. Mary is always correct," Ellis drawled as he stood slowly. "Your sister and I were just chatting while we waited for you."

Mary paled. Surely Ellis wouldn't mention the proposal before he had her answer.

"What about? More fashions?" Douglas chuckled

"No, but I believe I've found the source of so many of those inaccurate rumors that trouble me. You know, the ones we talked about yesterday."

"Really," Douglas said slowly, drawing out the word before he turned away to study the sideboard. "I'll need a drink for this."

Ellis glanced Mary's way, brow raised in question. She knew what he was asking her to confirm. He wanted to know her source of information and already suspected Douglas. It was true that every bad thing she'd ever heard about Ellis Worth had come from her own brother's lips. Douglas had often shared, boasted almost, that his best friend was an utter scoundrel when it came to women.

Mary nodded slowly, and Ellis faced Douglas again.

"It's been you all along," Ellis said.

"You can thank me later," Douglas said with a laugh. He refilled his glass without a trace of remorse and wore a smug smile that made her heart sink in shame.

Mary had never once questioned if such tales hadn't been an exaggeration. But Douglas had lied to her. "Why would you lie about a friend's behavior and cause so much mischief? You could have ended any discord between myself and Ellis if you had spoken truthfully about the man."

She'd always believed Douglas and kept her distance from Ellis unless that proved impossible. She had whispered warnings to other ladies to be on their guard around him too.

A sinking feeling began as Douglas stared blankly at them. "Why should what you feel matter to Worth?"

"It matters," Ellis disagreed, a dark scowl adding color to his cheeks.

"Oh, Ellis," she whispered. "What have I done to you?"

"Hush now." He held one hand out to her, finger pointing in a manner suggesting she should stay out of it. But it was all her fault mothers protected their daughters from the likes of him. She'd seen him snubbed with her own eyes, and at the time she'd been relieved to think that she'd spared an innocent woman a great deal of trouble.

Now she would like to sink through the floor in shame.

When Douglas turned around, Ellis was watching him. "Why?"

"Why what?"

"What did I ever do to deserve this treatment?" Ellis spoke very loudly, so out of character that Mary flinched. "What gave you the right to ruin my reputation so thoroughly that the duke would hear of it and send a warning through his bloody stuck-up solicitor?"

"Other men would be thankful for the help I gave you," Douglas replied, a dull flush rising up his neck to color his cheeks too. "Your name is on every delectable lady's lips."

"How could being gossiped about and falsely labeled a rake be helpful? Your own sister believes I was dared to swim across the Serpentine naked, but her understanding of the event is quite strange. There was no lover of mine standing on the sideline egging me on to prove my devotion to. There was only you, drunk and addled without a horse or your boots. One boot was sinking into the Serpentine, and the horse wisely fled your jug-bit theatrics."

Douglas's face grew set. "What harm was there in spreading a little-embellished tale now and then? The ladies do love to tame a rake, and you've had your share of offers."

"But none I ever wanted to take up. Good God, man, I have more sense and appreciation for women than you've ever given me credit for."

Mary moved to stand beside Ellis, worried the pair would come to blows because it was clear that Douglas had done his friend a huge disservice. She felt compelled to set the record straight. "Douglas, ladies from upstanding families avoid rakes unless they wish for a ruin that would leave them unmarriageable. I warned my friends away from Ellis based on your lies. Ellis could very well have lost the chance to fall in love, and all because of us. He did not deserve what we have done, and I am ashamed of myself, and of you too."

Ellis caught Mary's hand and squeezed. "You had every reason to believe your brother."

Douglas turned red. "What the hell is this? Get your hands off my sister, scoundrel, before I knock your block off."

Ellis released her.

"What is going on?" Mama asked from the doorway, eyes wide with fear as she took in the occupants of the room. Considering she was dressed in only her nightgown still and her cap was askew over her curls, their discussion had lured her from her warm bed. She hardly ever got up before eleven. "Why are you arguing with Mr. Worth at this hour?"

"Ellis is not a rake, Mama."

"Well, of course he is not. Mr. Worth is a fine gentleman, very courteous and kind. You would do well to emulate him, Douglas," Mama insisted.

A tense expression turned down Ellis's lips. "You're too kind Mrs. Vine, but I do not always behave as I should."

"That's not true, Ellis," Mary whispered. Ellis could have ruined her, but instead, he'd offered a marriage. An alliance Ellis would never have offered before the events of last night, though. He was a *good* man. "I have been so wrong."

He nodded briskly. "Our disagreements, fueled by Douglas's untruthful poison, are over. If you will excuse me, Mrs. Vine, Miss Vine, I came to say goodbye."

"What do you mean?"

"I've been summoned to Calder tomorrow to meet with the duke. I don't know when I will have leave to return to London." Ellis moved to stand before Douglas. "You'd better pray our paths do not cross again too soon, Mr. Vine. Next time I see you, you'd better have a bloody good apology prepared. We are not confidants anymore. I don't want your kind of help ever again."

He turned away, and Mary's heart sank like a rock.

Douglas followed Ellis a few steps. "I saved you from the parson's trap, you fool. Your future inheritance makes you irresistible to women. You're too young to know what you want, and you would have been easily trapped by some silly chit who never really wanted you for yourself."

Ellis's gaze flickered to Mary and away quickly. "What you failed to understand is that I always intended to marry young, coming to London for the season was in the hope of meeting the love of my life. I want a family again, a wife to love, and a home filled with laughter. I want to marry very, very much indeed."

"Are you mad? Family causes nothing but trouble. A bachelor's life is just the thing for you. Once the word is out, you'll have any woman you want."

"If you think I will stay in London for that, then you don't know me at all, and certainly don't deserve the family you have."

Ellis left quietly without glancing back.

Her mother marched into the room and punched her hands to her hips. "Douglas, the only trouble I see is you making a botch of all my plans. Did it never occur to you that Ellis might marry Mary? I was so looking forward to seeing Calder when he became a duke."

"Mama!"

Mama blushed. "A mother can hope, can she not? He'd make a very considerate husband, and he could be a duke one day."

Mary blushed. There was no chance of that now. "Mama, no."

"He *will* be the next duke," Douglas cut in as he rubbed his hands. "Sooner than I ever dreamed."

Mary took a step back, seeing her brother in an all new and unappealing way. "Why?"

"His cousins died. Worth is next in line." Douglas grinned. "He'll be back to London when he cools his head."

Mama clapped her hands. "How wonderful for him."

"Poor Ellis," Mary whispered. To lose what little family he had so suddenly. Admittedly he was not close to his cousins, but had spoken of them fondly many times.

"Yes, yes, poor, poor Ellis Worth. You'd think he'd be happy, but he cannot see the advantage. Ungrateful wretch." Douglas scowled. "He can have any woman he wants now and it's not enough. Go back upstairs, Mama, and let me manage things."

"I may as well. Mr. Worth will never speak to us again after this," Mama complained. "I shall miss his visits."

Mary's mind raced. A future duke would not keep up a connection with someone who disparaged him. Mary may be forgiven, but she'd likely never see him again because of Douglas.

After last night she could easily see herself married to Ellis, sharing his bed, getting to know the real man whose kisses left her breathless.

The gaping hole left behind after his departure broke her heart. He sounded so lonely. So disappointed. Betrayed by a friendship that was almost family. She'd never even had a chance to answer his unexpected proposal.

It was not right to leave that question unanswered forever. Mary had to see Ellis again before he left London and there was only one way an unmarried lady could call on a bachelor.

There was no doubt about it. She'd have to break a few more rules today.

CHAPTER SEVEN

ELLIS STRODE HOME IN A FUNK. His best friend had cursed his life. The meddling, idiotic fool! Without ever consulting him or discussing the matter, Douglas had made him practically evil in Mary's eyes. The only thing Ellis had going for him was his future elevation, something that made him exceedingly angry right now. He hardly wanted to be married for that reason alone. He'd prefer it if his future wife actually liked him.

He burst into his modest home and slammed the door shut behind him so hard, the paintings on the walls rattled.

Brown, his elderly butler, immediately shuffled into the hall to see what was amiss. "Sir?"

"It's just me."

The old fellow relaxed. "I thought perhaps we'd had a caller and I'd not heard the knock fast enough again."

"No, no callers." And possibly none ever again of the kind he'd like.

He took a deep, cleansing breath at the unappealing prospect of what sort of visitors he might expect to receive in the future. There would also be invitations, blatant advances, new acquaintances with agendas. Never more would society think of him as just Ellis. He'd forever be known as a future duke and hunted.

"If there is nothing else, sir?"

"No, there's nothing more I need."

He was so ready to marry and quite depressed by today's disappointment that he sank down onto the first flight of steps.

Love had slipped through his fingers. Admittedly Ellis had not been sure he had Mary's affections, but he'd felt hope as he stared at her blushing face when they'd come face-to-face that morning. He had feared he'd imagined the attraction between them, but it had burned hot the moment she'd stepped into the drawing room. So hot he'd had to taste her sweet lips again. To touch her and be touched. He had been prepared to offer marriage to make up for last night and ended up offering her his whole heart too when he'd proposed.

He wanted her trust and her love.

He didn't want her to be impressed by anything but the man he really was.

He tossed away his hat and gloves, careless of where they landed despite the fact that they were the very best he had. Today had gone well until Douglas had barged in.

He leaned forward, and set his chin on his hand and stared ahead without actually seeing anything. Damn Douglas for his addled machinations to spare him being considered husband material. He'd done his job so well that Mary had believed the worst of him for years. Would knowing the truth have brought them together? The woman hardly ever changed her mind once it was set. He might never win Mary, but at least she'd had all the facts in her possession now.

And maybe, just perhaps if she did not love him at all, she might send the woman who could care for him into his path one day.

Rap, rap, rap.

He didn't bother to lift his head as his

butler returned, shuffling slowly toward the door. It couldn't be anyone he wanted to see anyway. He'd just sit here and wait to be overrun by eager callers. Nothing had changed. He was exactly the same man as he'd been before his uncle's solicitor had informed him of his new future.

"No, wait!" Brown called out in outrage.

Ellis lifted his head at the outburst and found himself staring straight into Mary's beautiful eyes. He sighed at the sight of her red hair falling out of its moorings. "Mary," he whispered, sure he was dreaming this lovely interruption to his depression.

"Are you all right?" she asked, peeling her gloves off as she hurried over.

"Am I all right?" He shook his head. "Not really."

"Then perhaps this might help." She placed her hands on either side of his head and kissed him full on the lips. "There."

The kiss was too brief to soothe, but it was a start. "There what?"

Her frown was immediate. "I just kissed you."

"And quite nicely, but what does it mean, Mary?"

"Scandal is what it implies, sir, if you don't mind my opinion?" Brown grumbled as he limped back to his post beneath the stairs. "Best watch out, or you'll be on your way to the altar."

Mary grinned after the butler. "I certainly hope so, Brown."

Ellis stood slowly, pulling Mary close. "What do you mean by that?"

She smiled. "I do like you, Ellis, but I never liked the things Douglas said you'd done."

"I'm decidedly annoyed with your brother right now. I have also to explain something that is essential and unavoidable."

"You're the next Duke of Levinson. I know."

He winced. "I wanted to tell you myself."

"I apologize on my brother's behalf if I was not supposed to know, but really, what was the harm in telling us? You've been part of the family for so long. I must admit I was a little thrown by your cousins' deaths and annoyed by Douglas being so happy about it. It's hard to know what to say, but I don't believe you're eager for the title."

"No, I am most assuredly not. Douglas

has no idea what I really want for my life. All he sees is the income I'll have in the future, and the estate. A future that is probably very far away, I do hope. My great uncle is in perfect health, and he was always kind if a little distant."

"You'll make a generous duke one day," Mary said, cupping his face. "You can marry any woman you want."

His heart sank again, and he closed his eyes. "Is that why you are saying yes to me? Because one day you'll be a duchess?"

"Of course not, silly," Mary laughed and pulled. She dragged him into his study and closed the door. "I said yes because I do want to be with you in public, but I especially want to be with you in private. Society only accepts that sort of thing if we're married or going to be."

She untied the sash on her gown and tied the two door handles together. "That ought to hold for a while, should anyone have followed me," she mused. "Now where were we?"

He backed toward the chaise, stunned by the wicked glint in her eye. If she was attempting to seduce him, it was working. He was beginning to feel rather excited by what might happen next with her. "Should I call for someone to save me?"

"Why would you want to do that?" She paused, boldly eyeing him, and then glanced down at herself. "Hmm, we have far too many clothes on for what I have in mind."

She lifted her hands to her bodice, and his breath caught as she commenced to undress, flinging her clothing left and right until all that remained was a thin shift and corset.

Growing hot, he loosened his cravat. "Your reputation will be in tatters if anyone learns you were alone with a known rake."

His words of caution did not prevent him removing his boots and breeches. He fumbled with the buttons on his waistcoat and shirt as Mary drew near, provocatively swinging her hips a little. She rested her warm little fingers on his chest and caressed his pectoral muscles in the exact same manner she had last night. Proving his identity didn't have the least impact on her fascination. "For the first time, you might actually be one, or is it me who's the rake, and you're the innocent I'm about to seduce?"

"The latter I hope," he said hoping she meant to do just that.

Mary smiled, shoved him backward onto the chaise, and sank down on his knees. "I'll need help to get naked."

He pressed his lips to her shoulder, unable to believe his luck. Mary meant to have him. Right now and forever. "Hmm, I recall we both seemed to enjoy being naked."

"It was lovely. Dear Ellis, hurry."

"Yes, Devi." He made short work on the lacings, and when undone, set his hands on her bare hips. He swept his hands upward, taking the clothing as he caressed her lush body.

Naked now, she swiveled around to face him. "Centurion," she sighed.

"Lead me astray, into all sorts of rakish wickedness, and let me worship you." He drew her closer, struggling not to shout out his happiness. "Only you."

Mary twined her arms about his neck. "Only me," she agreed.

"I live to serve." He kissed her lips boldly, stroking his tongue into her warm mouth. She brought his hand to her breast, and he laughed at her happy little moan. "Patience, goddess, you'll never be denied my devotions now."

"My hero," she sighed, quite dreamily, and it was music to his ears.

Ellis eased her to the cushions, and then he settled over her carefully. He grinned down at her flushed face. "This position seems vaguely familiar."

Mary widened her legs, took him in hand, and drew him up until the head of his cock nestled against her sex. "There, that is where we stopped last night."

His head spun for a full moment. Mary and the bold goddess of last night were one and the same. He'd lose control if he let her have her way right now so he caught her hand and raised it above her head.

"We stopped for an excellent reason," he said, brushing the tip of his cock against her slick folds to tease her. "Neither of us knew what we were about to do."

Knowing only seemed to heightened his desire and anticipation.

"That reason does not exist today." Slipping free of his grip to brush fingertips over his shoulders and upper arms in the most flattering way imaginable. "I know exactly who you are, Ellis James Worth."

"Who am I?"

"The man who understands me better than I know myself. The man who finally let me see who he really was but only after I'd made a complete fool of myself."

"We made a wicked pair last night," he whispered, capturing her breast in one hand and pinching the nipple lightly to drag a tortured whimper from her lips.

"You were right that a rake would have taken my virtue last night and left me to face the consequences alone. But you didn't abandon me. You made me wait until I could decide with a clear head what I want in my life. I want you so much. I went to that ball looking for the love of my life and there you were—waiting for me to notice you properly." She grinned and looped her arms around his neck, pulling him closer. "Make love to me, Ellis. Make me yours."

"It could easily become the deepest love, I think, if we always turn to each other and stop listening to gossip." He caressed her body until she shivered against him. "I'm willing to risk my heart if you will have me," he said.

"I will take very good care of your heart and mine." Mary kissed him hard, fingers tangling in his hair tightly. He was taken aback when she gripped his backside and pulled him in but he didn't resist. He entered her slowly, amazed by her slick heat on the head of his cock. She hissed a little but then turned her face to his for kisses that never seemed to stop. Mary curled her arms tightly about his shoulders as he began to move, and smiled up into his face. "Your love and understanding is what I long for most."

"I love you today, Mary," he confessed pausing his lovemaking to gather her close against his chest. "And for the rest of my life, too."

The End

DISTINGUISHED ROGUES SERIES

Chills ∼ Broken ∼ Charity

An Accidental Affair ∼ Keepsake

An Improper Proposal ∼ Reason to Wed

The Trouble with Love ∼ Married by Moonlight

Lord of Sin ∼ The Duke's Heart

Romancing the Earl

One Enchanted Christmas

Desire by Design ∼ His Perfect Bride

Pleasures of the Night ∼ Silver Bells

Seduced in Secret ∼ Yours Until Dawn

*

SCANDALOUS BRIDES

Wicked with Him

Desperately Seeking Seduction

Love and Other Disasters

WILD RANDALLS SERIES

Engaging the Enemy ~ Forsaking the Prize

Guarding the Spoils ~ Hunting the Hero

*

SAINTS AND SINNERS SERIES

The Duke and I ~ A Gentleman's Vow

An Earl of Her Own ~ The Lady Tamed

*

REBEL HEARTS SERIES

The Wedding Affair ~ An Affair of Honor

The Christmas Affair ~ An Affair so Right

*

MISS MAYHEM SERIES

Miss Watson's First Scandal

Miss George's Second Chance

Miss Radley's Third Dare

Miss Merton's Last Hope

ABOUT THE AUTHOR

USA Today Bestselling Author Heather Boyd believes every character she creates deserves their own happily-ever-after—no matter how much trouble she puts them through. With that goal in mind, she writes steamy romances that skirt the boundaries of propriety to keep readers enthralled until the wee hours of the morning. Heather has published over fifty regency romance novels and shorter works full of daring seductions and distinguished rogues. She lives north of Sydney, Australia, with her trio of rogues and a four-legged overlord.

Learn more about Heather at:
Heather-Boyd.com

www.ingramcontent.com/pod-product-compliance
Lightning Source LLC
Chambersburg PA
CBHW031031190726
48286CB00003BA/1128